For Cedric Tolley —J.W.

For Teresa —B.B.

The 39 Apartments of Ludwig van Beethoven

Jonah Winter

Pictures by Barry Blitt

schwartz & wade books · new york

FACT: Ludwig van Beethoven was born in the town of Bonn in the country of Germany in the year 1770.

Years later, he became a great composer.

FACT: Ludwig van Beethoven owned five legless pianos and composed great works on the floor.

FACT: Ludwig van Beethoven lived in **39** different apartments—which is of course the subject of our story. (See book title.)

But now things get fuzzier. Did our hero really pour water on top of his head while composing? Why did he live in so many different apartments? And what were those apartments like?

As far as we can tell, Beethoven's first apartment was a beautiful parlor in the center of Vienna, which is the capital of Austria. Here, it seems, he composed the "Moonlight" Sonata and his First Symphony.

But—
Ludwig forgot to
pay the rent.

So—he was kicked out.

This was a problem, because . . .

FACT: It is very difficult to move a piano.

FACT: It is even more difficult to move five pianos.

After two centuries of research, we still have no clues as to how all the pianos made it from one apartment to the next. Nor can we be certain that the following sentence is true, but here it is: Ludwig van Beethoven's next home was a basement apartment in a dangerous part of town. Here he composed Piano Sonatas 3 through 17, his Violin Concerto in D Major, and the Second Symphony.

Why did Ludwig move after only eight and a half days?
Was it, as his diary suggests, because of the "hideous stinky
cheese smell" that filled his apartment? We do not know.

Nor do we truly know how the pianos made it out of the building. But scuff marks discovered in the hallway can mean only one thing: The pianos must have been slid through the back door, then drawn up to the roof by a system of pulleys

and lowered onto a second-floor balcony at the front of the building, where the neighbors must have been kind enough to allow the movers to wheel the pianos through their apartment to the stairway,

down

the

stairs,

and out the front door.

It is unclear how the pianos made it into Ludwig van Beethoven's next apartment, which was like a palace—full of light and air. From the terrace he had a view of the Danube River, and it is likely that the smell of Viennese coffee wafted in through his open windows.

Here he composed Symphonies 3 through 5, Piano Sonatas 18 through 23, and many chamber works for clarinet, bassoon, oboe, flute, and English horn, in addition to several string trios. It was indeed a busy time.

But Ludwig van Beethoven was going deaf, and he had to bang quite loudly on the five pianos to hear anything. Much research has revealed that there were complaints from the neighbors about the noise. Bits of paper with the German words for "SHUUUUUT . . . UP!!!" have been discovered. And then there are the dents in the ceiling of his downstairs neighbor—probably made by a broomstick banged repeatedly. Poor Ludwig was again kicked out.

By now the movers were certainly getting fed up. In the diary of one Anselm Schwartz, we find the following, translated here into modern English: "After this move, I'm out of here. That dude is WHACKED in the head! Yow. . . . My back is, like, REALLY messed up!"

The records do show that this job was a humdinger. The easy part was moving the pianos out—they were simply lowered from the balcony, and all went smoothly. The hard part was moving the pianos into the new apartment—which was tiny, and in an attic.

It seems the movers had to push the pianos

through the old castle next door,

through a
grand hall
displaying suits
of armor,

up three flights of stairs,

and into a dentist's office. The movers then BASHED IN the wall (a theory supported by the gaping hole we have found behind a poster with the German words for "Don't forget to floss" that must have been hung to conceal the spot). They passed through the dentist's apartment,

out into the hallway,

and up onto Ludwig van Beethoven's new roof,

where they could be lowered carefully, then hoisted into his
tiny attic apartment, which, luckily, had an enormous window.

Here Beethoven wrote all his piano concerti, as well as his famous *Pastoral* Symphony (no. 6). It was gorgeous music, but repeated complaints were filed with the local magistrate—mostly by one neighbor, a certain Fräulein Inge Hausfrau. In one complaint, she demands the maestro's immediate arrest because "that madman is banging on those blasted pianos day and night!"

And yet, it appears that Ludwig could hardly hear his pianos at all. After much growling and pouring of water over his own head, he quite likely decided that there *must* be something wrong with this apartment. It was time to move once again.

Probably because it had been so much work getting the pianos into this apartment, Ludwig van Beethoven decided to leave them. He needed some new pianos anyway, since the old ones weren't loud enough anymore. (Or so he thought.)

By now, Beethoven's hearing had gotten so bad that when he played his new pianos in his stylish new "loft-style" apartment—HE PLAYED BANGINGLY LOUD! This notion is supported by a startling discovery made in his neighbors' apartments: Hundreds of cotton balls with traces of dried earwax. Clearly, the noise was unbearable.

And the neighbors must have been furious: Scraps of an old eviction notice show that Ludwig van Beethoven was booted after only one day.

It should be noted, however, that during that one day he composed ten violin sonatas, two more symphonies, and one more string quartet. It seems to have been a good place to work.

Not surprisingly, the great composer
was somewhat upset at being kicked out.
"DON'T THESE FOOLS KNOW WHO I AM?!"
he scrawled on the bathroom wall.

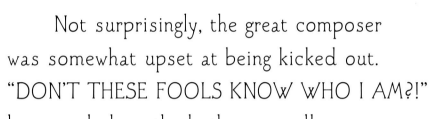

(Stains reveal that he then
dumped another bowl of
water on his head.)

Certainly the movers had lost all patience with schlepping Ludwig's many pianos up and down stairways. A diagram has been found, clearly drawn by mover Schwartz and revealing a new plan in which the pianos would never have to *touch the ground.* A large slide would be constructed—much like a cement truck's enormous funnel.

The movers must have studied the bold plan carefully before attempting it.

The slide would stick out the window and extend all the way to a chimney several blocks away. The pianos would slide **out** the window **toward** the chimney, where a catapult would **shoot** them **up** into the air.

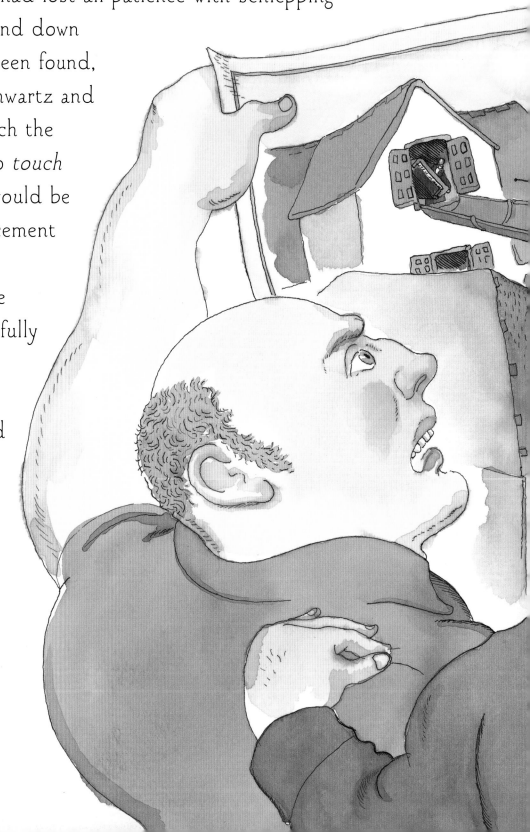

The pianos would then fall straight through a hole in
the ceiling of Ludwig van Beethoven's new apartment, where a
gigantic piano-sized pillow would cushion their fall.

But, according to various eyewitness accounts and newspaper articles from that day, the entire device blew away in a storm.

FACT: That's all we know of the **39** apartments of
Ludwig van Beethoven.

AUTHOR'S NOTE

Ludwig van Beethoven was in fact a great composer who lived from 1770 to 1827. As an adult, he did in fact live in the great musical city of Vienna in the great musical country of Austria. It is also true that he lived in no fewer than **39** apartments during his adult life in and around Vienna! And: He owned SEVERAL LEGLESS PIANOS . . . !

However, very little is known about the apartments themselves—or about Beethoven's difficulties in moving his many pianos in and out of them. Therefore, this story picks up where history leaves off. Why *did* Beethoven change apartments so often? How *did* he move his pianos in and out of the various buildings he lived in? *Were* there frequent complaints from the neighbors?

There is evidence that neighbors' complaints would have been warranted: According to the accounts of people who visited Beethoven in his apartments, he made quite a racket while composing his masterworks. He howled, growled, and repeatedly poured water on his own head. As his deafness got worse—for he did in fact go deaf—his playing got louder. During the last several years of his life, when he was completely deaf, he banged on the piano keys with the fury of a madman. Eyewitness accounts tell us that Beethoven did in fact lose his mind. It's no wonder: How must it feel to be one of the greatest composers of all time . . . and then to go deaf? That Beethoven composed his greatest work, the Ninth Symphony, after he had completely lost his hearing is nothing short of miraculous. That he managed to compose so much beautiful music while constantly moving his pianos in and out of different apartments may be short of miraculous—but it *is* something to think about.

(The endpapers of this book are details from a facsimile of a recently rediscovered piano composition that had been missing since 1890, the "Grosse Fuge," written in Beethoven's own hand. It is unclear just *where* Beethoven composed this work, or how many neighbors were disturbed in the process. And what was this work doing at the bottom of a library drawer in Pennsylvania for more than a hundred years? This too is unclear. . . .)

A photograph of a detail from a working manuscript score for the piano transcription of the
"Grosse Fuge" in B flat major, Op. 134, appears on the endpapers. This landmark work was
written in Beethoven's own sprawling hand in brown and black ink, sometimes over pencil,
with thousands of deletions, corrections, erasures, and smudged alterations, during his last
summer, 1826. Used courtesy of Sotheby's Picture Library, London.

Beethoven
(youngish)

Copyright © 2006 by Jonah Winter
Illustrations copyright © 2006 by Barry Blitt
All rights reserved.
Published in the United States
by Schwartz & Wade Books,
an imprint of Random House Children's Books,
a division of Random House, Inc., New York.
SCHWARTZ & WADE BOOKS and colophon
are trademarks of Random House, Inc.
www.randomhouse.com/kids
Educators and librarians,
for a variety of teaching tools, visit us at
www.randomhouse.com/teachers
The text of this book is set in Aged.
The illustrations are rendered in
pen-and-ink and watercolor.
MANUFACTURED IN CHINA
2 3 4 5 6 7 8 9 10
First Edition

Library of Congress Cataloging-in-Publication Data
Winter, Jonah.
The 39 apartments of Ludwig van Beethoven / Jonah Winter ;
illustrated by Barry Blitt.- 1st ed.
p. cm.
Summary: Ludwig van Beethoven and his five legless pianos
keep having to move from one apartment to another when his
neighbors complain about the noise.
ISBN-10: 0-375-83602-0 (trade)
ISBN-10: 0-375-93602-5 (lib. bdg.)
ISBN-13: 978-0-375-83602-2 (trade)
ISBN-13: 978-0-375-93602-9 (lib. bdg.)
1. Beethoven, Ludwig van, 1770-1827–Juvenile fiction.
[1. Beethoven, Ludwig van, 1770-1827–Fiction.] I. Title:
Thirty-nine apartments of Ludwig van Beethoven.
II. Blitt, Barry, ill. III. Title.
PZ7.W75477Aacj 2006
[E]–dc22
2005031232